POR...

AN IMPORTANT MESSAGE TO T READER FROM KING ALVIN

Dear Reader and most loyal friend,

As one of my closest and most trusted knights, I am sending you on a mission of the greatest importance. All is not well at Portcullis Castle. Reports have reached me that the lord of the castle, Baron Toadfettle, has turned against me and has hatched an evil plot.

According to my sources, the Baron has either taken, or is about to take, one of my knights prisoner. I have no idea which one it might be, as my knights are fighting in all four corners of the Earth.

You must enter Portcullis Castle through a secret passage and make contact with the magician Haggard. Though trusted by Baron Toadfettle he is, in fact, a loyal friend of mine. Together, you must find out <u>who is the prisoner of Portcullis Castle.</u>

Do not fail me, brave knight. The wars abroad do not go well, and I must keep peace here in my own land. I am relying on you.

King Alvin.

This book was written by
Phil Roxbee Cox & Rupert Heath

photographed by
Sue Atkinson
and designed by
Joe Pedley.

The series editor was
Gaby Waters.

With thanks to
John Russell & Jo Litchfield

On every double page, there are questions that need to be answered. These are there to keep you thinking and to help you find out just what's going on at the castle. When you've reached page 41, you should be able to say who the prisoner is. If you get stuck, there are hints on page 42, answers on pages 43 to 47, and the solution is on page 48.

1

Spell 133

FOR ESCAPING FROM ANYWHERE
To escape from anywhere
  you will need:
A bird's feather
A drop of red candle wax
A rusty nail
A Vandusian snail

Place them all in a row,
Shout out where you want to go . . .
And you'll be free!

Spell 13

BEARD
To leng
  follow
A bearde
Some stro
Four horses
Much luck

Attach the ho   s
beard with the
clockwise three
saying: 'Fol-d
today this bear
LONGER!' Then
galloping as fa

STAR
SOCIETY
for Magicians,
wizards, Warlocks

Musical potion
for Lady Olivia
(This should
improve
her frightful
lute-playing.)

Haggard
Magician
People-into-Toads
a Speciality

The Magician's Lair

Time: Monday, a little before three o'clock
Place: Haggard's room in Portcullis Castle

The secret passage has brought you out here, into a room packed with every kind of magical potion you can imagine, and crawling with snails and toads. Suddenly, there's a puff of green smoke. It's Haggard, the king's friend and secret enemy of the evil Baron Toadfettle. There's powerful magic at work here!

Where does Haggard get his magical powers from?

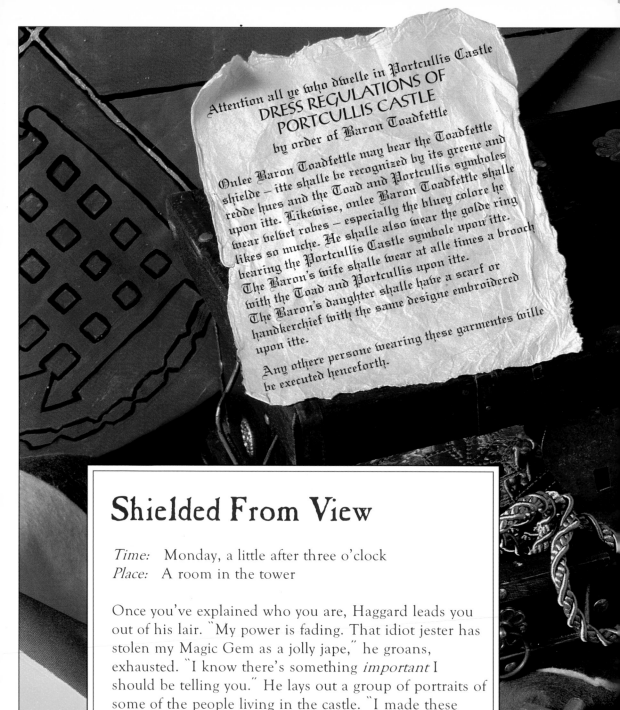

Attention all ye who dwelle in Portcullis Castle

DRESS REGULATIONS OF PORTCULLIS CASTLE

by order of Baron Toadfettle

Onlee Baron Toadfettle may bear the Toadfettle shielde – itte shalle be recognized by its greene and redde hues and the Toad and Portcullis symboles upon itte. Likewise, onlee Baron Toadfettle shalle wear velvet robes – especially the bluey colore he likes so muche. He shalle also wear the golde ring bearing the Portcullis Castle symbole upon itte.

The Baron's wife shalle wear at alle times a brooch with the Toad and Portcullis upon itte.

The Baron's daughter shalle have a scarf or handkerchief with the same designe embroidered upon itte.

Any othere persone wearing these garmentes wille be executed henceforth.

Shielded From View

Time: Monday, a little after three o'clock
Place: A room in the tower

Once you've explained who you are, Haggard leads you out of his lair. "My power is fading. That idiot jester has stolen my Magic Gem as a jolly jape," he groans, exhausted. "I know there's something *important* I should be telling you." He lays out a group of portraits of some of the people living in the castle. "I made these pictures using a machine from the future called a camera," he yawns. He suddenly falls, snoring, to the floor. You study the pictures.

Can you put a name to every face?

The Baron's food taster

The Baron's jester

Food For Thought

Time: Monday, just gone four o'clock
Place: The castle kitchen

Leaving the power-drained magician in a deep sleep, you disguise yourself as a servant and slink into the kitchens. This is probably as good a place as any to pick up Castle gossip. You carry some carrots over to an enormous table and begin to peel them. "I've lost my ring!" screams a man in a high-pitched voice. You recognize the Baron's food taster, Sir Clifford. "It must have come off when I was inspecting the food. A gold piece for anyone who finds it!"

Can you find the missing ring?

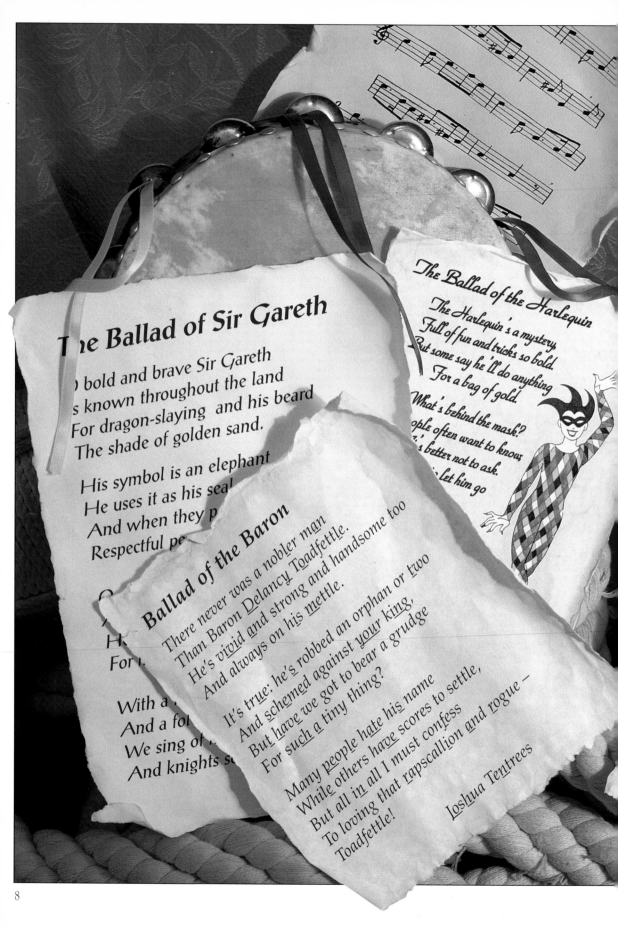

The Ballad of Sir Gareth

O bold and brave Sir Gareth
s known throughout the land
For dragon-slaying and his beard
The shade of golden sand.

His symbol is an elephant
He uses it as his seal
And when they p
Respectful pe

H
For t

With a
And a fo
We sing of
And knights s

The Ballad of the Harlequin

The Harlequin's a mystery,
Full of fun and tricks so bold.
But some say he'll do anything
For a bag of gold.

What's behind the mask?
ople often want to know
's better not to ask.
Let him go

Ballad of the Baron

There never was a nobler man
Than Baron Delancy Toadfettle.
He's vivid and strong and handsome too
And always on his mettle.

It's true: he's robbed an orphan or two
And schemed against your king,
But have we got to bear a grudge
For such a tiny thing?

Many people hate his name
While others have scores to settle,
But all in all I must confess
To loving that rapscallion and rogue –
Toadfettle!

Joshua Tentrees

Music, Music, Music!

Time: Monday, sometime after six o'clock
Place: The minstrels' gallery

No gold piece from Sir Clifford for finding his ring,
just a clip around the ear! But he did mention that
there's to be a special banquet later tonight in the
castle's great hall. Still disguised as a servant, you take a
quick look at the hall from up in the minstrels' gallery.
There's no one around, but you spot a coded message.

What does it say?

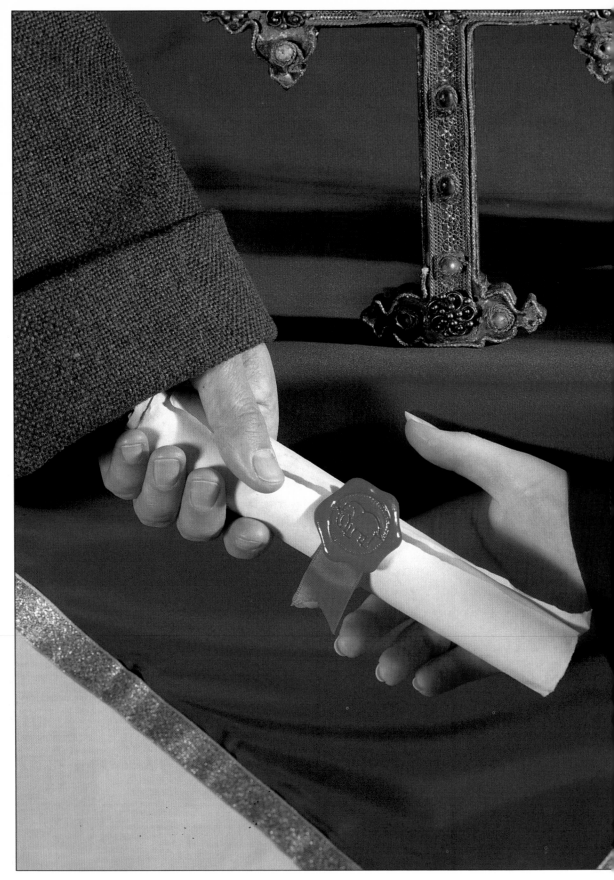

In The Chapel

Time: Monday, at the stroke of seven
Place: The castle chapel

The coded message in the minstrels' gallery has led you
here. You're squeezed behind a cold stone pillar, out of
sight. The only other people in the chapel are a monk,
wearing a simple brown habit, and a girl in flowing
robes. From your hiding place, you can't see their faces.
"Were you followed, Lady Olivia?" asks the monk.
"No," replies the lady, her face still in shadow. He
hands her a sealed letter.

Who is the letter from?

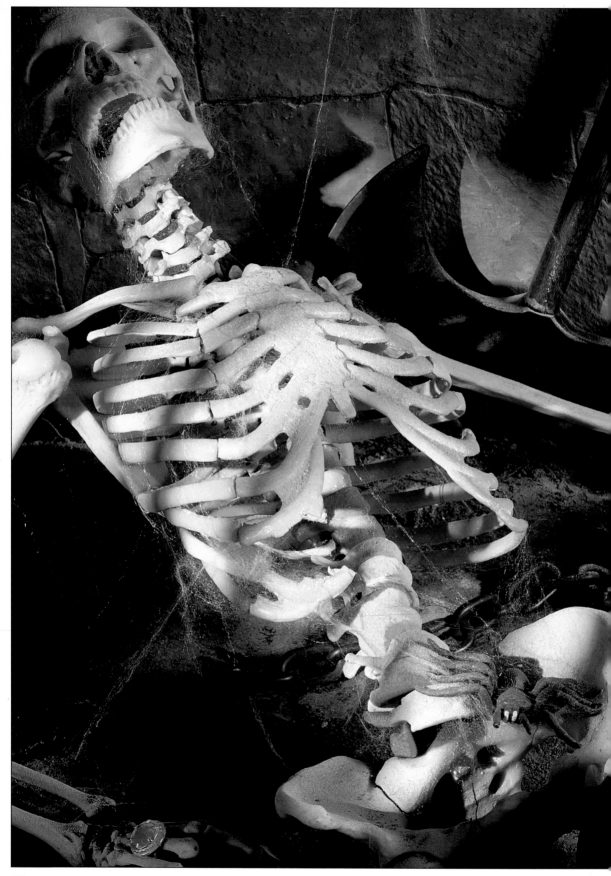

Smelling A Rat

Time: Monday, a quarter after eight o'clock
Place: Outside the dungeon

If the letter comes from Sir Gareth, could he be the
prisoner? If he is, he isn't being held down here. The
place is empty – except for a very old skeleton, a flea-
ridden rat and some hungry looking cockroaches.
Maybe Baron Toadfettle hasn't actually taken his
prisoner yet. Maybe he's still waiting to pounce. Or
maybe the prisoner is being held in another part of the
castle. Your thoughts are distracted by a familiar sight.

What is it?

Feasting Your Eyes

Time: Monday, eight o'clock
Place: The castle's great hall, during a banquet

You've hurried here from the dungeon. You don't want to miss any speeches Baron Toadfettle might make. Disguised as a squire this time, you help to serve the food. "A toast!" cries the Baron, getting to his feet. "To King Alvin . . . and to one of his closest friends, a *guest* in Portcullis Castle!" He laughs and throws himself back into his chair, grabbing a piece of meat. You spy a key on a gold chain around his neck.

Where have you seen a key like that already?

Possible Prisoners

1. Sir Gareth,
2. Sir Flaxen,
3. Sir Joan,

Sir Flaxen

Loyal knight to King
Nickname: Wanderer
Main characteristic:

...bouts

...fo

Sir Gareth

Loyal knight to King
Nickname: Goldenbea...
Main characteristic:
disgustingly high level
of chivalry
Present whereabouts:
Unknown
History:
Son of Arthur
Leschampes of
Summerfield
Became an app...
King Alvin at th...
H... ...ought f...
seve... foreign wars

...n of Jacob and Saran
... Flaxen became King
...ever knight at the
...just ten years old. Since
...alongside the king on
...mpaigns, gathering
...t every opportunity.
...the battlefield
...f Katmandu, in
...amel lost their

My lord,
    Please keep this missive safe for it
containeth secret information for your
eyes only.
    The DRAGON is now ready to
be released — ready to spit fire and
strike fear into the hearts of all Baron
Toadfettle's enemies! Please come to its
secret chamber and witness for yourself
its lethal potential.

        Long live Baron Toadfettle!
Down with King Alvin!

        Sir Lee of Grimthorp
        Master of the DRAGON

16

Sir Joan
Loyal knight to King Alvin
Nickname: The Lioness
Main characteristic:
Hates traitors
Present whereabouts:
Believed fighting for the K...
History:
Her father (now dead) w...
King Alvin's and now Sir Joan...
in his footsteps. She ran away from hom...
twelve to join King Alvin's army and became
his first female knight, one of the king's
...t and most loyal followers.

Secret Papers

Time: Monday, sometime soon after eight o'clock
Place: Baron Toadfettle's private chamber

Having taken Baron Toadfettle's spare key, you've
tiptoed past a sleeping guard to see if it unlocks the
door to the Baron's private chamber. Success! On a
table are some papers. One is a list headed '𝔓𝔬𝔰𝔰𝔦𝔟𝔩𝔢
𝔓𝔯𝔦𝔰𝔬𝔫𝔢𝔯𝔰' with the names of four of King Alvin's loyal
knights on it, and *yours* is the fourth! There are reports
on all four of you but, for some reason, yours is blank.
Could one of the others have already been taken
prisoner? And what's this about a DRAGON?

Have you spotted anything to do with dragons elsewhere?

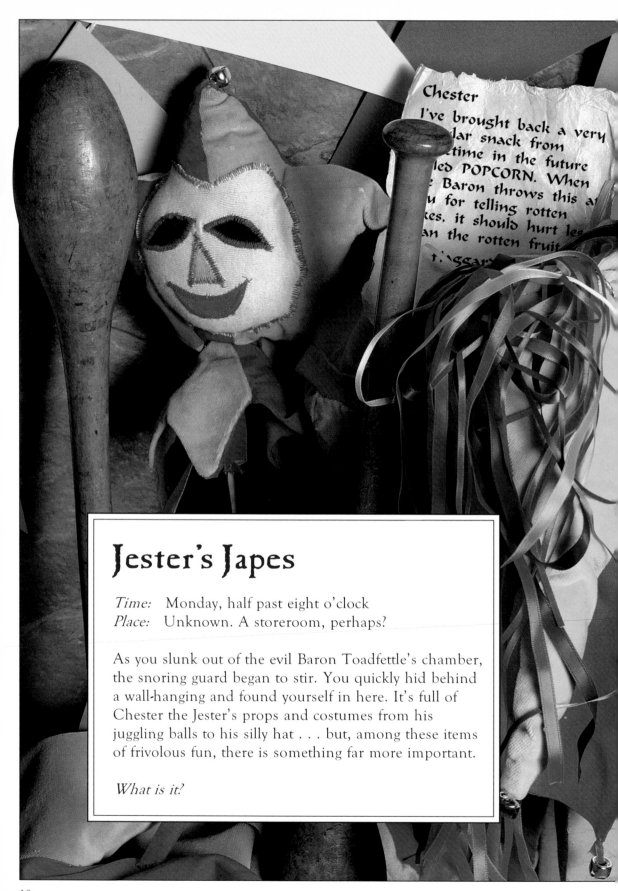

Chester
I've brought back a very
...lar snack from
...time in the future
...led POPCORN. When
... Baron throws this at
...u for telling rotten
...es, it should hurt les...
...an the rotten fruit
...t. iggar...

Jester's Japes

Time: Monday, half past eight o'clock
Place: Unknown. A storeroom, perhaps?

As you slunk out of the evil Baron Toadfettle's chamber,
the snoring guard began to stir. You quickly hid behind
a wall-hanging and found yourself in here. It's full of
Chester the Jester's props and costumes from his
juggling balls to his silly hat . . . but, among these items
of frivolous fun, there is something far more important.

What is it?

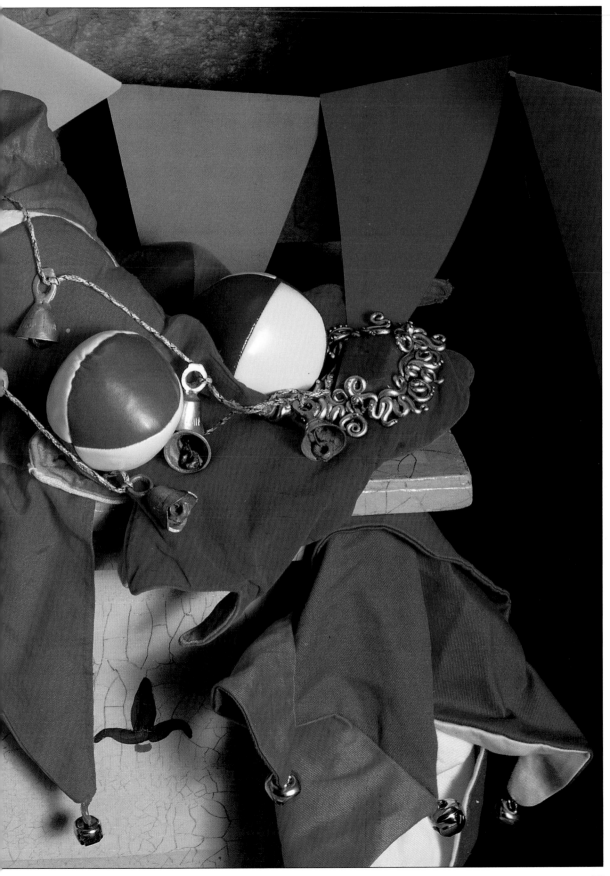

Let The Joust Begin

Time: Tuesday, early morning
Place: The jousting tent

You've given Haggard the Magic Gem but he still can't tell you who the prisoner of Portcullis Castle is. "I *know* there's something important I forgot to tell you," the wizard yawns, "but it'll take more than one night for my full powers to return."

He helps you to disguise yourself as a knight visiting the castle for the day's joust. "Keep the visor of your helmet down and call yourself the Green Knight," he says. "The evil Baron Toadfettle welcomes all jousting knights. No one will question why you're here." You are only half-listening. You've spotted a vital piece of information lurking among the weaponry.

What is it?

Sir Gawain's

Sir John's

The Baron's
HANDS OFF

THE ORDER OF JOUST:
1. Sir John of Lockwood AGAINST
   Robin, Comte de Jeune
2. ~~Sir John~~ AGAINST   Killed in battle
   Sir Gawain de Aquitaine
3. The Black Knight' AGAINST
   'The Green Knight'
4. 'The Glum Knight' AGAINST
   'The Happy Knight'

The Game's Afoot

Time: Tuesday, midday
Place: Under Baron Toadfettle's chair at the joust

Ducking under a flap at the back of Baron Toadfettle's tent, you find yourself face-to-heel with the Baron who is seated on a raised platform. "King Alvin has a spy in the castle," Sir Clifford whispers in his ear. "Just as you predicted would happen. We found a secret passage from the village that must have been used as the way in." There's no doubt it's *you* they're talking about, but you're distracted by a crumpled note on the ground.

Who is 'the Wanderer' mentioned in this note?

Long winter...
mail underwear, 1 pa...
Full metal jacket, 1
previous owner, very
good condition (a few
small arrow holes)
Contact
...umblestone

REMINDER TO ALL PERSONNEL

The Room Without Locks, at the top of the West Tower, has a sprung door that is easy to open from the outside but, once opened, automatically swings shut and stays shut. 'Tis not possible to open it from within. BE CAREFUL!

FOUND: ONE GAUNTLET RETRIEVED FROM A VAT OF BOILING OIL.

All contestants in the ...pcoming Tug-of-War ...with the soldiers of ...alliard Castle should ...t to the ...room for ...ard's special ...ening potio...

DIRECT ATTACK WAGON

No mention of the Direct Attack Wagon may be made by name. This highly secret weapon, being made up of a mighty bombard, or cannon, mounted upon wheels and disguised to appear like a covered wagon or cart, must only be referred to by the agreed codename. Any soldier failing in this d... will be put to death.

By Order of BARON TOADFETTLE

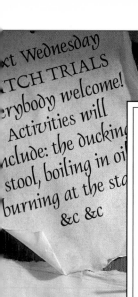

Orders Of The Day

Time: Tuesday, five minutes past the hour of one
Place: The Guard Room

Sweating inside your Green Knight's disguise, you wonder what to do next. You're running out of time. The Baron knows you're inside the Castle! You must find out which of the king's loyal knights, shown on the list in the baron's chamber, is the prisoner . . . then get away from here as soon as possible. With all the guards on duty at the joust, you sneak a look in the Guard Room. Along with the general regulations is an explanation of what the Castle 'dragon' really is.

What is it?

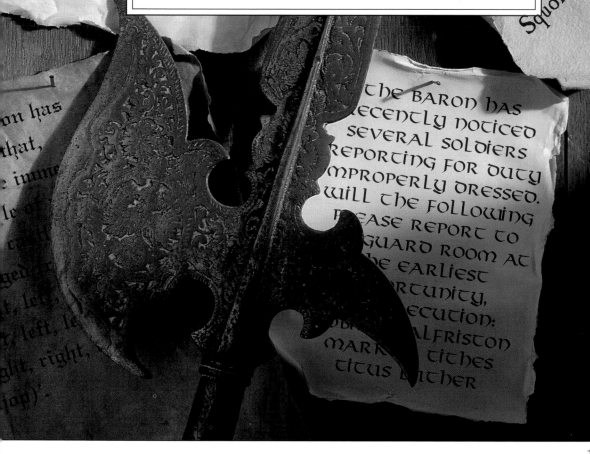

My Lady's Chamber

Time: Tuesday, just before two o'clock
Place: Lady Olivia's chamber

With everyone at the joust, you search in here. Sir
Gareth is loyal to King Alvin and, if he's writing to
Olivia in secret, perhaps she can be trusted . . . but
first you need to know what was in his letter to her.
The Baron may be evil and an enemy of the king, but
that doesn't mean to say that his daughter has to be.

Where is the letter she was handed in the chapel?

LAVENDER
BLOSSOM

My one love, my joy, my life, I am still months away from Portcullis Castle, fighting [...] king in a far-off land. [...] long to be close to [...]more! How sad I [...]oyalty to King [...]us from sharing our [...]enly! [...]Until we meet again, my lily-white dove, my peach!

Your loving Gareth

28

Hidden Letters

Time: Tuesday, two o'clock
Place: Lady Olivia's chamber

You read Sir Gareth's letter to the Baron's daughter and the odd reply that she has yet to send him. Sir Gareth's letter is embarrassing though it makes it clear that he's a long way from Portcullis Castle. But what if he comes here? King Alvin did write that the Baron has 'either taken, or is *about* to take, one of my knights prisoner'. Then you spot a hidden message in Olivia's reply.

What does it say?

...areth,
    there once was a famous castle
with a Keep full of soldiers, to keep
Away enemies From abroad. The
armies kept on coming but couldn't
breach the Castle walls. You May
well imagine that to Become a
soldier in the castle was A great
privilege, and the greatest thing a
soldier could do was to single-
handedly capture a Prisoner.
            Olivia

Rugs
the Sulta
of Azil

Spices
from
Empire
Alexa

All the best,
Haggard

Present Dangers

Time: Tuesday, sometime after two o'clock
Place: A room off the courtyard

Still disguised as the Green Knight – and with the visor firmly down over your face – you boldly walk around the Castle courtyard which is being used for the joust. You enter a room full of gifts for the Baron, and study the treasures. "Hail, Green Knight," a familiar voice calls out behind you. It's the food-taster. "Hail, Sir Clifford," you reply, the words echoing inside your closed helmet. "Welcome to Portcullis Castle," the little man continues. "Who will you be riding against today?" You have to think fast.

Who is your opponent supposed to be?

RA
FRC
OUI
HA

From Prince Henry

Exotic seeds

Magic Beans

Precious gems

Even more precious gems

Spices from the Orie

31

Pay Sir Clifford 5 pieces of gold belching cordial and stomach pills

Portcullis Castle Monthly Account

Executioner	20 pieces
Sergeant at Arms	10 pie
Chief spy	1 b
Murderers	2 pi
Food for hungry hounds	
Jewels for Baroness	
Harlequin	

each

s of gold

NIL

1 bag of gold

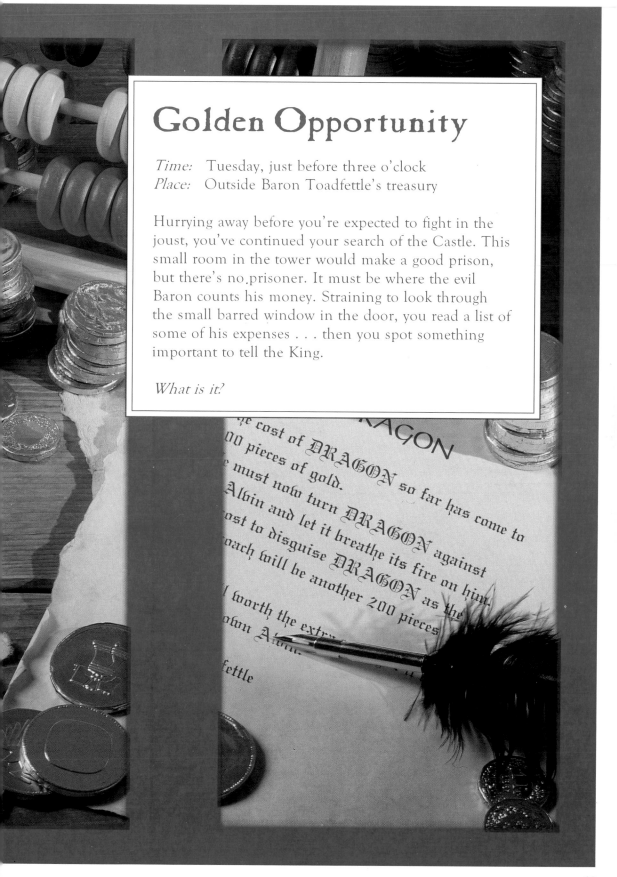

Golden Opportunity

Time: Tuesday, just before three o'clock
Place: Outside Baron Toadfettle's treasury

Hurrying away before you're expected to fight in the joust, you've continued your search of the Castle. This small room in the tower would make a good prison, but there's no prisoner. It must be where the evil Baron counts his money. Straining to look through the small barred window in the door, you read a list of some of his expenses . . . then you spot something important to tell the King.

What is it?

ᴿAGON

e cost of DRAGON so far has come to
00 pieces of gold.
e must now turn DRAGON against
Albin and let it breathe its fire on him.
ost to disguise DRAGON as the
oach will be another 200 pieces
l worth the extr
ᴼᵒn Albin.

fettle

A Dog's Life

Time: Tuesday, sometime after three o'clock
Place: The Castle kennels

You've read about hungry hounds in the castle accounts. Perhaps one is guarding the prisoner? A trip to the kennels might help. The building appears to be empty. You lift your visor to take a closer look . . . and see someone lying in the straw! Drawing your sword, you step forward. "I know who you are," chuckles a voice from the straw. "We can't talk here. Meet me on top of the east tower at nightfall. Until then, let me sleep."

Who do you think the man in the straw is?

FANG

To The Battlements

Time: Tuesday, after dark
Place: The battlements of the east tower

Dressed as a squire, and wearing a fake bushy beard, you're reading a note from the mysterious man in the straw. It's attached to an arrow that just whistled past your ear in the darkness — narrowly missing you — as you waited for him to meet you on the ramparts as promised. In the flickering candlelight you can see that, for once, it's a message that isn't in code! If what it says is true, the end to your quest is in sight.

But where is the Room Without Locks?

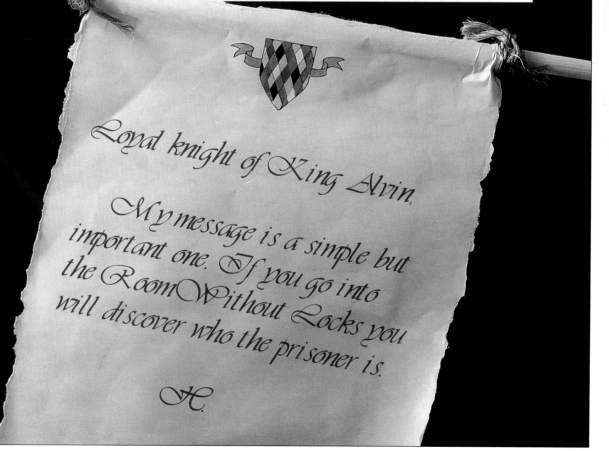

Loyal knight of King Alvin,

My message is a simple but important one. If you go into the Room Without Locks you will discover who the prisoner is.

H.

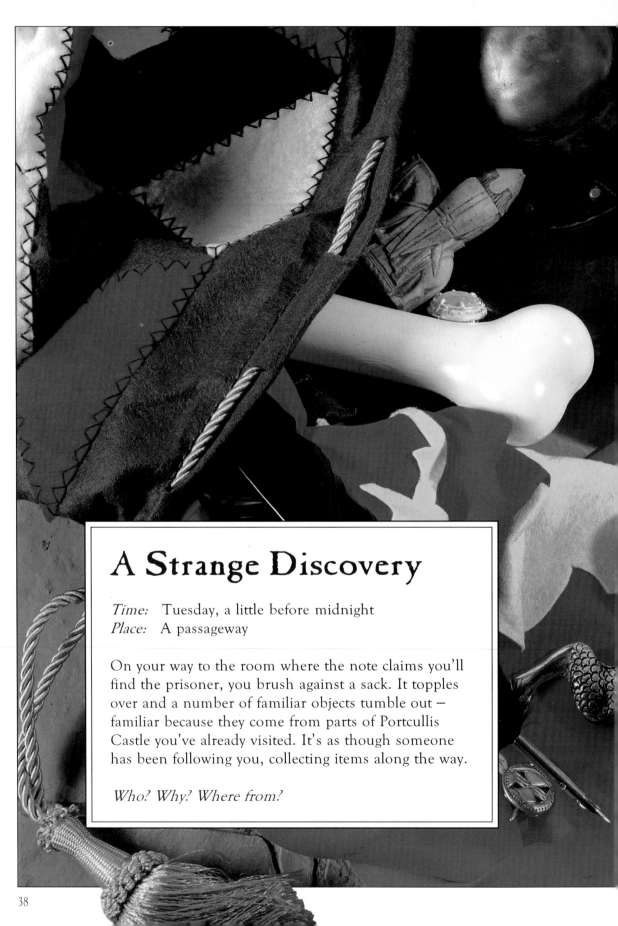

A Strange Discovery

Time: Tuesday, a little before midnight
Place: A passageway

On your way to the room where the note claims you'll
find the prisoner, you brush against a sack. It topples
over and a number of familiar objects tumble out –
familiar because they come from parts of Portcullis
Castle you've already visited. It's as though someone
has been following you, collecting items along the way.

Who? Why? Where from?

LAVENDER
Blossom

ddings and Parties

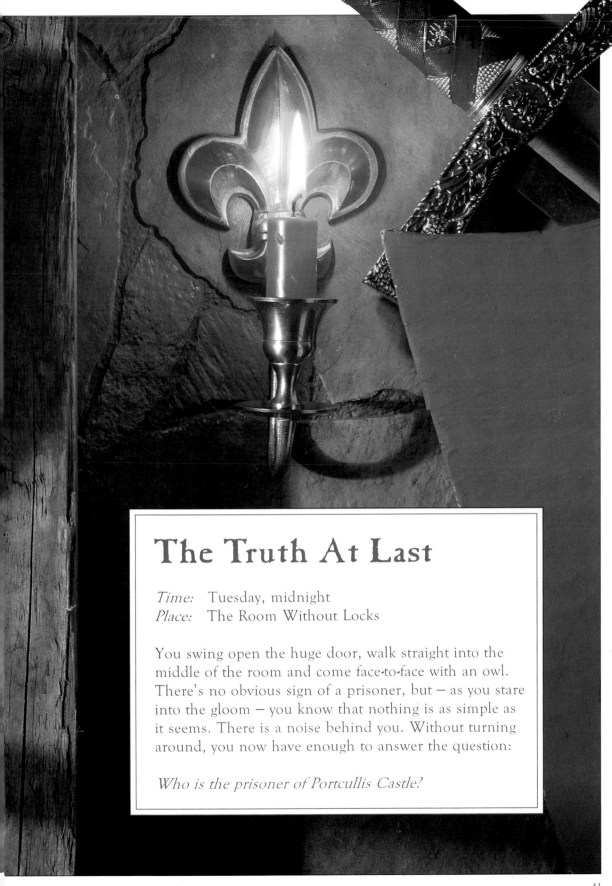

The Truth At Last

Time: Tuesday, midnight
Place: The Room Without Locks

You swing open the huge door, walk straight into the middle of the room and come face-to-face with an owl. There's no obvious sign of a prisoner, but – as you stare into the gloom – you know that nothing is as simple as it seems. There is a noise behind you. Without turning around, you now have enough to answer the question:

Who is the prisoner of Portcullis Castle?

The Helpful Hints

Pages 2 & 3
The reason's in a rhyme.

Pages 4 & 5
Any notions from Haggard's potions? The dress regulations should help you with the rest.

Pages 6 & 7
Here's a golden opportunity to use your eyes.

Pages 8 & 9
The answer is underlined.

Pages 10 & 11
An elephant might seal the identity of the letter writer.

Pages 12 & 13
The skeleton will lend you a hand in solving this puzzle.

Pages 14 & 15
Pages 4 & 5 will unlock the mystery.

Pages 16 & 17
There's more than one kind of dragon in this story . . .

Pages 18 & 19
What did Haggard say the jester had stolen?

Pages 20 & 21
Your suspect list has just shortened.

Pages 22 & 23
The Wanderer was last seen on pages 16 & 17.

Pages 24 & 25
Could DRAGON be short for something?

Pages 26 & 27
Look for the elephant again.

Pages 28 & 29
It stands out — in capitals!

Pages 30 & 31
The answer's in *black* and white on pages 20 & 21.

Pages 32 & 33
What is the DRAGON to be used for?

Pages 34 & 35
There's a clue at your fingertips — and at his!

Pages 36 & 37
Go back to pages 24 & 25 for a Reminder.

Pages 38 & 39
The bag tells you who and the who tells you why.
Match every item in the picture with locations you have visited already.

Pages 40 & 41
You should know enough about the Room Without Locks to figure this out on your own . . .

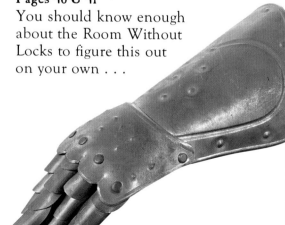

The Answers

Pages 2 & 3

Haggard gets all his magical powers from his Magic Gem. In a poem on page 3, Haggard says that the Magic Gem's **'sparkle is the source of all the power I need.'**

Pages 4 & 5

We know the names of the Baron's food taster and jester from papers on Haggard's table (page 3). The food taster is called Sir Clifford. The jester is called Chester.

The other three people can be recognized from the 'DRESS REGULATIONS OF PORTCULLIS CASTLE'. We know only the Baron is allowed to wear a blue velvet robe and a gold portcullis ring. Therefore the man standing in front of the Toadfettle shield must be Baron Toadfettle himself. The two women in the other picture can be identified in the same way. The Baron's wife, Baroness Toadfettle, is the one wearing the Toadfettle brooch and his daughter, Lady Olivia, is the one holding a handkerchief with the Toadfettle emblem on it.

Pages 6 & 7

The green and gold ring is hidden here.

Pages 8 & 9

The coded message is hidden in the '***Ballad of the Baron***' on page 8. To decode the message, read only the underlined letters. Once all the other letters have been removed, the message says:

LADY OLIVIA, I MUST SEE YOU IN THE CHAPEL AT SEVEN. FRIAR JOHN.

Pages 10 & 11

The letter bears a seal of an elephant. From the '*Ballad of Sir Gareth*' on page 8 we know that '*his symbol is an elephant, he uses it as his seal*'. Therefore this letter is most probably from him.

Pages 12 & 13

The skeleton is wearing a ring very similar to the one you found for Sir Clifford on pages 6 & 7! Actually this isn't the same one. Although it's the same design, it's much older and dirtier. Maybe this skeleton is one of Sir Clifford's ancestors — maybe he displeased one of the Baron's!

Pages 14 & 15

The key around Baron Toadfettle's neck is identical to the one lying on the table on page 4. It must be important.

Pages 16 & 17

You have come across three dragons so far in the story.

The first is mentioned on page 3 on a label on Haggard's table. He describes Baroness Toadfettle as an '*old dragon*' — but he's just being rude about her!

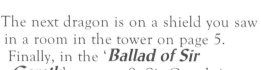

The next dragon is on a shield you saw in a room in the tower on page 5. Finally, in the '*Ballad of Sir Gareth*' on page 8, Sir Gareth is said to '*be known throughout the land for dragon-slaying*'.

Keep your eyes open for more dragons later.

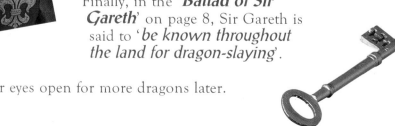

Pages 18 & 19
Lying well-camouflaged on a piece of red cloth is . . . Haggard's Magic Gem!

You learned on page 4 that Chester the Jester had stolen the Magic Gem. Now that you've found it you can return it to Haggard and maybe restore his magical powers.

Pages 20 & 21
On the paper headed 'THE ORDER OF JOUST' it states that Sir Joan has been '*killed in battle*'. She was one of the four possible prisoners on pages 16 & 17. You can cross her off your list of possible prisoners now.

Pages 22 & 23
You've seen the name '*The Wanderer*' once before: on the paper about Sir Flaxen on page 16. 'The Wanderer' is his nickname. The note says that '*the Wanderer is still in foreign lands*'.

Pages 24 & 25
The notice on page 24 headed '**DIRECT ATTACK WAGON**' has certain letters bolder than the others. If these letters are taken alone they spell '**D-R-A-G-O-N**'. The so-called Dragon you keep hearing about is a shortened form of '**DIRECT ATTACK WAGON**' – a '**highly secret weapon**' which is 'disguised to appear like a covered wagon'.

Pages 26 & 27
The letter is here.

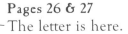

Pages 28 & 29

To decode the hidden message in Olivia's letter, read only the words beginning in a capital letter. The message then says:

Gareth,
Keep Away From The Castle.
You May Become A Prisoner.
Olivia.

Pages 30 & 31

You have to think back to *'THE ORDER OF THE JOUST'* on page 21. It says that the Black Knight is to joust against the Green Knight. As you are the *'Green Knight'* (for the moment at least!) your opponent must be the Black Knight.

Pages 32 & 33

There is a piece of paper in the treasury on page 32 which contains more information about DRAGON. The part that you can read talks of disguising DRAGON as King Alvin's coach. It is signed by Toadfettle himself. It sounds as if he intends to use DRAGON against the King! It is vitally important that his majesty learns this as soon as possible.

Pages 34 & 35
Those pretty fingernails should give you the
vital clue. It's the Harlequin, whose
fingernails match his diamond-patterned suit.
You saw his ballad (and picture) on page 9.
Be wary of trusting him — remember the
words of that ballad!

Pages 36 & 37
There is a notice about the Room Without
Locks in the Guardroom on page 24. The notice,
headed '**REMINDER TO ALL PERSONNEL**', tells you that the
Room Without Locks is 'at the top of the West Tower'.

Pages 38 & 39
The bag on page 39 is the give-away clue to
the thief's identity. The pattern matches
the suit of the Harlequin, a known trickster
who will '*do anything for a bag of gold*'. In the
Baron's Treasury on pages 32 & 33 the
Portcullis Castle
accounts state that
the Harlequin has
been paid one
bag of gold — so
must be
working for
Toadfettle. It
looks as
though he's
been following

you, helping himself to items from around the
castle as he went.

And you want to know where each item in the
picture has come from? You'll have to find that
out for yourself.

Pages 40 & 41
How many people are left on your
list of possible prisoners?
You may have more time than you
bargained for to work out the
solution . . .

The Solution

According to the letter from King Alvin on page 1, Baron Toadette "has either taken, or is about to take one of my knights prisoner." According to the papers in the evil Baron's chamber on pages 16 & 17, Toadette had narrowed it down to capturing one of four of the king's most trusted knights: Sir Flaxen, Sir Gareth, Sir Joan, or – believe it or not – you!

You know from the crumpled note on pages 22 & 23 that 'the Wanderer is still in foreign lands,' and from pages 16 & 17 that the Wanderer is another name for Sir Flaxen. If Sir Flaxen is abroad, then he can't be the prisoner.

The letter on pages 28 confirms that Sir Gareth is also 'many months from the castle', so he can't be the prisoner either.

And what of Sir Joan? Sadly, according to the 'order of joust', in the tent on pages 20 & 21, Sir Joan has 'died in battle', – which also makes this knight very unlikely to be the prisoner!

So who is the prisoner of Portcullis Castle? Why, you are, of course. That noise behind you, on pages 40 & 41, was the door slamming shut. That's the trouble with the Room Without Locks. It doesn't need them. According to a notice in the Guard Room on pages 24 & 25, the room has a 'sprung door that is easy to open from the outside but, once opened, automatically swings shut and stays shut. 'Tis not possible to open from within.' You walked into a trap. This was the important thing Haggard kept forgetting to tell you!

By leaking the story that he was about to seize one of the king's loyal followers, Baron Toadette was making sure that the king would send one of his most trusted knights to investigate . . . and that the investigator – who turned out to be you – would become the very prisoner you were sent to find!

You know from his conversation with Sir Clifford on pages 22 & 23 that the Baron was aware that the king's spy was in the castle. At the banquet, he was referring to you when he gave a toast 'To King Alvin . . . and to his friend, a guest at Portcullis Castle', though he didn't know, then, which of the king's loyal knights you actually were.

The Harlequin recognized you (from your photo on page 17) on pages 34 & 35, however, when you had your visor open and your undisguised face showing. He even said so. We know from the ballad in the minstrels' gallery, on pages 8 & 9, that the Harlequin would 'do anything for a bag of gold', . . . and we can see from the accounts in the evil Baron's counting house, on pages 32 & 33, that Toadette has paid him that.

Once Harlequin knew who you were – a knight on Toadette's list and one the king himself described as 'one of my closest and most trusted knights', – he happily led you into the trap.

All is not lost

All the ingredients you need for a spell to escape from anywhere can – fortunately for you – be found in the Room Without Locks. All you need to do is remember the spell, follow the instructions and you should be free. Then you can warn King Alvin about the Baron's secret weapon, the 'DRAGON'.

First published in 1997 by Usborne Publishing Limited, Usborne House, 83-85 Saffron Hill, London EC1N 8RT, England.
© Copyright 1997 Usborne Publishing Ltd.
The name Usborne and the device are Trade marks of Usborne Publishing Ltd. All rights reserved.
No part of this publication may be reproduced, stored in any retrieval system, or transmitted in any form or by any means, electronic, mechanical, photocopying, recording or otherwise, without the prior permission of the publisher.
Printed in Spain   U.E. First published in America August 1997